Wayne was a lumpy piece of wood.
He said, "My shape is just no good.
All my friends are smooth and neat,
but I'm just rough from head to feet."

1

Wayne said, "I'll just go away."
He walked all night. He walked all day.

Then Wayne came to a sudden stop.
He had found an amazing shop!

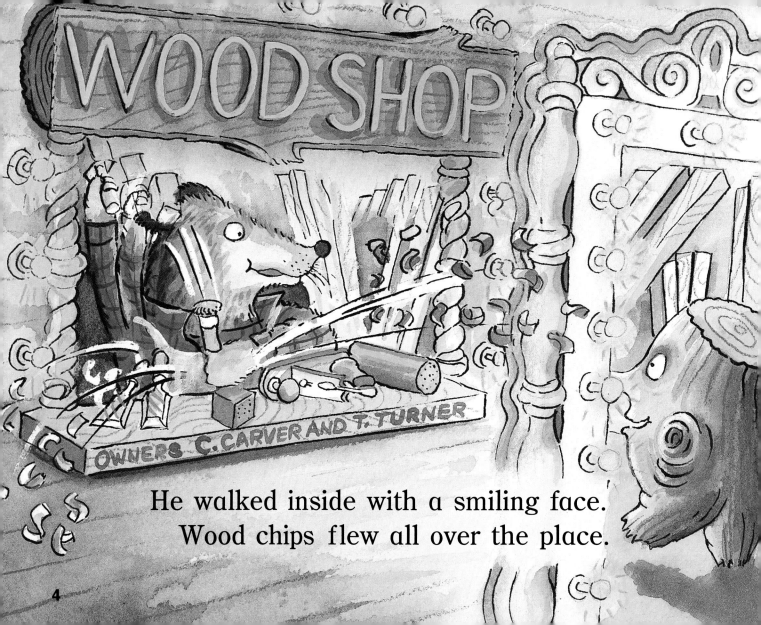

He walked inside with a smiling face.
Wood chips flew all over the place.

OWNERS C. CARVER AND T. TURNER

WOOD SHOP

Wayne was soon a different shape.
"Wow," he said. "I feel just great!"

Then the carvers worked some more.
Now Wayne could roll along the floor.

7

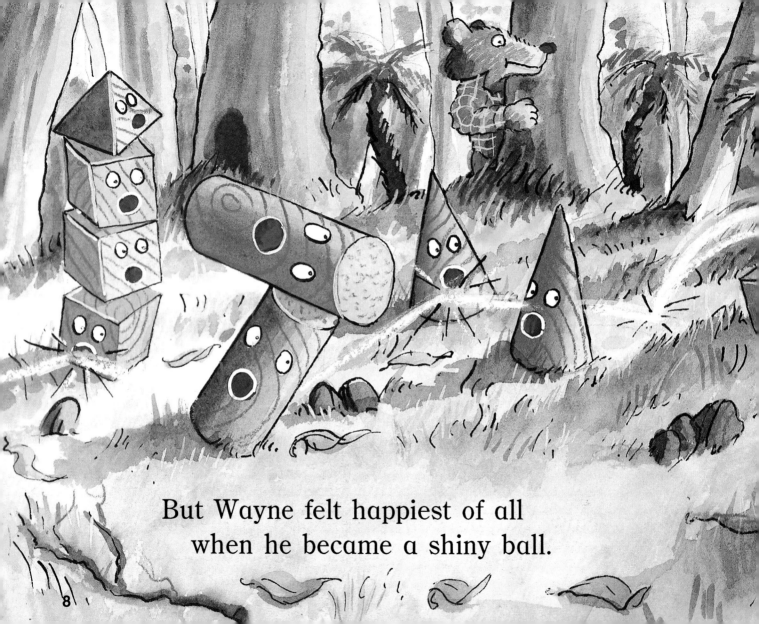

But Wayne felt happiest of all
when he became a shiny ball.

WAYNE'S NEW SHAPE

WRITTEN BY
CALVIN IRONS

ILLUSTRATED BY
PETER SHAW